The Tale of Boris
A Fable of the Red-tailed Hawk

It was early morning in the huge forest where the old cottonwood tree stood tall among the other trees. A large nest rested in the top of this tree, and morning awakened the Hawk family who lived in this nest. There was Mother Hawk, whose name was Calurus, Father Hawk, whose name was Buteo, and Borealis Hawk, the youngest member of the family. Mother and Father Hawk called Borealis, ''Boris,'' for short.

Boris was very curious and longed to soar from his nest to explore the forest.

Many sounds and sights could be investigated, and his heart pounded at the thought.

The Tale of Boris
A Fable of the Red-tailed Hawk

Written by John Mooy

Illustrated by Jane Stroschin

To our fathers,

Nat and Robert,

who taught us to see
not only with our eyes,
but also with our hearts.

ISBN 1 - 883960 - 06 - 1

Henry Quill Press
J.H. Stroschin
7340 Lake Drive
Fremont, Michigan 49412-9146

"Now don't go too far," Mother said. "The forest is such a large place, and you are so young; you could get lost."

Young Boris leaped from the nest to a nearby branch, pausing for just a moment before testing his wings. As he felt a gentle wind blowing through the forest, he launched himself from his perch. He soared among the clouds and the blue sky, gliding effortlessly while looking at the ground below. "Flying is just wonderful," he thought, getting further and further away from home.

The first thing to catch Boris' attention was a young rabbit which hopped quickly across an open field and disappeared into the cover of the tall oak trees. ''What must it be like to be able to jump so easily across a field?'' young Boris thought.

He soon forgot all about the rabbit as he spotted a mother deer and two fawns eating the leaves from a tree. ''Deer are certainly graceful, gentle-looking creatures,'' Boris thought as he continued his easy sail across the late morning sky.

Back in the cottonwood tree Mother Hawk gave screeching calls to Boris that went unanswered.

Circling high above, Boris became interested in something he had never seen before. A farmer named Mr. Pippen was standing next to a barn dipping a paint brush into a bucket. He moved the brush back and forth across the wooden side of the barn. Where the brush touched the wood it left a bright red streak of color.

Boris was amazed at how hard Mr. Pippen worked. Time passed quickly as Boris circled and circled and watched Mr. Pippen.

Mrs. Pippen appeared on the front porch of their white farmhouse, put her cupped hands to her mouth, and called, ''Mr. Pippen, it's time for lunch.''

Mr. Pippen put his bucket on a nearby fencepost and placed his brush in a bucket on the ground. He took a handkerchief from his back pocket, dried the perspiration from his forehead, and walked toward the house. Boris heard the slam of the door as Mr. Pippen disappeared inside.

Boris stretched his wings wide and let the wind do all the work as he floated down toward the barn for a closer look.

He perched himself on the tallest fencepost and felt something very strange! There was a wet, sticky feeling on his talons and his tail.

Boris turned his head and screeched, ''Oh no!'' He had perched on the edge of Mr. Pippen's paint bucket, and his tail was dipped into the paint. Would he be in trouble when he got home.

Boris decided to fly as fast as he could, thinking the paint would be blown off his tail. He flew straight up into the sky, but the faster he flew, the quicker the paint dried.

"Will I ever be in trouble!" he kept saying to himself as he climbed above the tops of the trees and headed home.

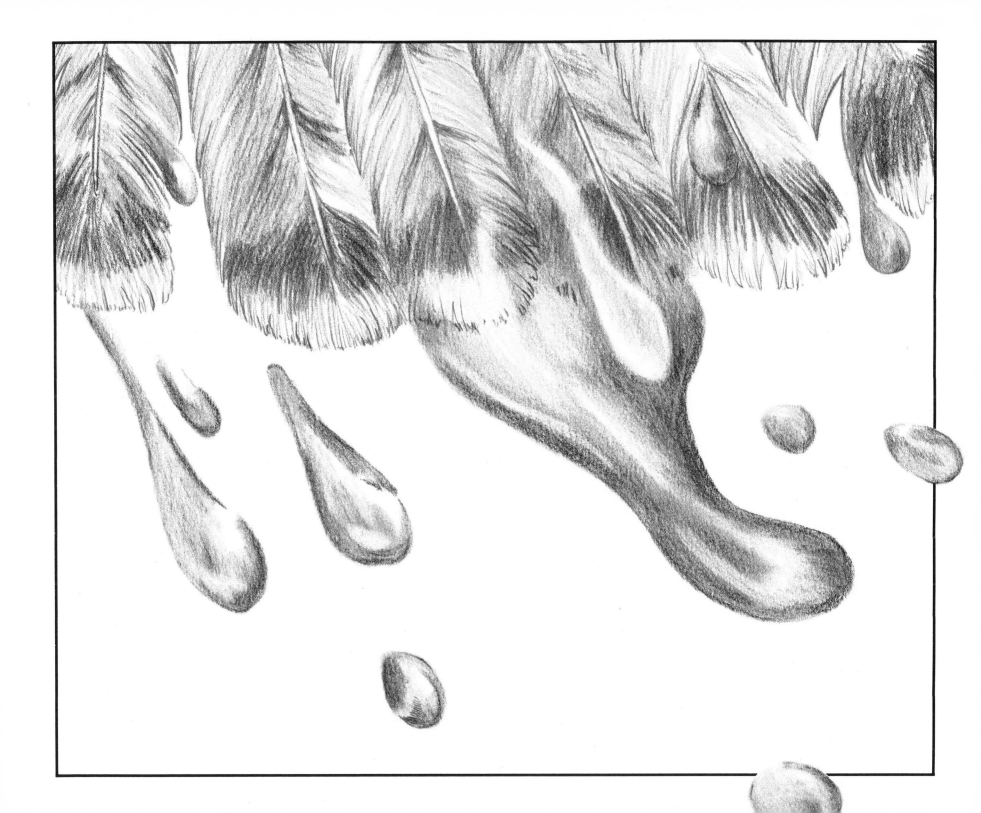

As he flew faster and faster, his Mother and Father came into view sitting on the edge of the nest.

Boris glided up to the nest and perched beside them, waiting to hear the worst. He had gone too far from home, and he was late for lunch, but that didn't seem so bad when compared to the look of his tail. Boris glanced back at his tail. He couldn't believe it. His curiosity had gotten him into big trouble.

Father Hawk began to speak. ''I'm not sure how you did it, but your Mother wasn't worried at all. When you soared above the trees, she spotted that beautiful red tail immediately. Even though you were further away than ever before, she knew where you were. From now on, because you're so easily seen, you will be able to explore almost anywhere.''

Even today, all the hawks in Boris' family have a red tail so that their parents can see them when they are far away.

The thing for you to remember is this: UNLESS YOU HAVE A BEAUTIFUL RED FEATHERED TAIL, IT IS BEST TO TELL SOMEONE WHERE YOU ARE GOING WHEN YOU LEAVE HOME.